llama llama mad at mama

Clearance
LAYAWAY
Discou
Instant coupon
TAKE ONE
20 %
OFF
Y
W!
ATER
Red Tag
Special !
Ai

llama llama
mad at mama

Anna Dewdney

SCHOLASTIC INC.
New York Toronto London Auckland Sydney
Mexico City New Delhi Hong Kong Buenos Aires

Llama Llama
having fun.
Blocks and puzzles
in the sun.

Time to shop!
It's Saturday!
Llama Llama
wants to **play.**

First the shopping, then a treat. Mama Llama gets the seat.

Llama dreaming
in the car—

Wake up! Wake up!
Here we are!

Great big building,
great big signs.
Lots of aisles,
lots of lines.

Llama Llama
out with Mama
shopping at the Shop-O-Rama.

SALE!
50 % OFF
BLUE DOT

SALE!
SALE!
SALE!

Yucky music,
great big feet.
Ladies smelling way too sweet.
Look at knees and stand in line.

Llama Llama
starts to **whine.**

SALE
20% OFF

Clearance sales
and discount buys.
What is little llama's size?
Try it on and take it off.
Pull and wiggle,
itch and cough.

Shirts and jackets,
pants and shoes.
Does this sweater
come in blue?
Brand-new socks
and underwear?

Llama Llama does not care.

Cheezee Puffs and Oatie Crunch.
What would llama like for lunch?
Llama Llama doesn't know.
Llama Llama wants to **go.**

Loaf of bread
and Cream of Wheat.
Llama Llama wants his treat.
It's no fun at Shop-O-Rama.
Llama Llama
MAD at Mama!

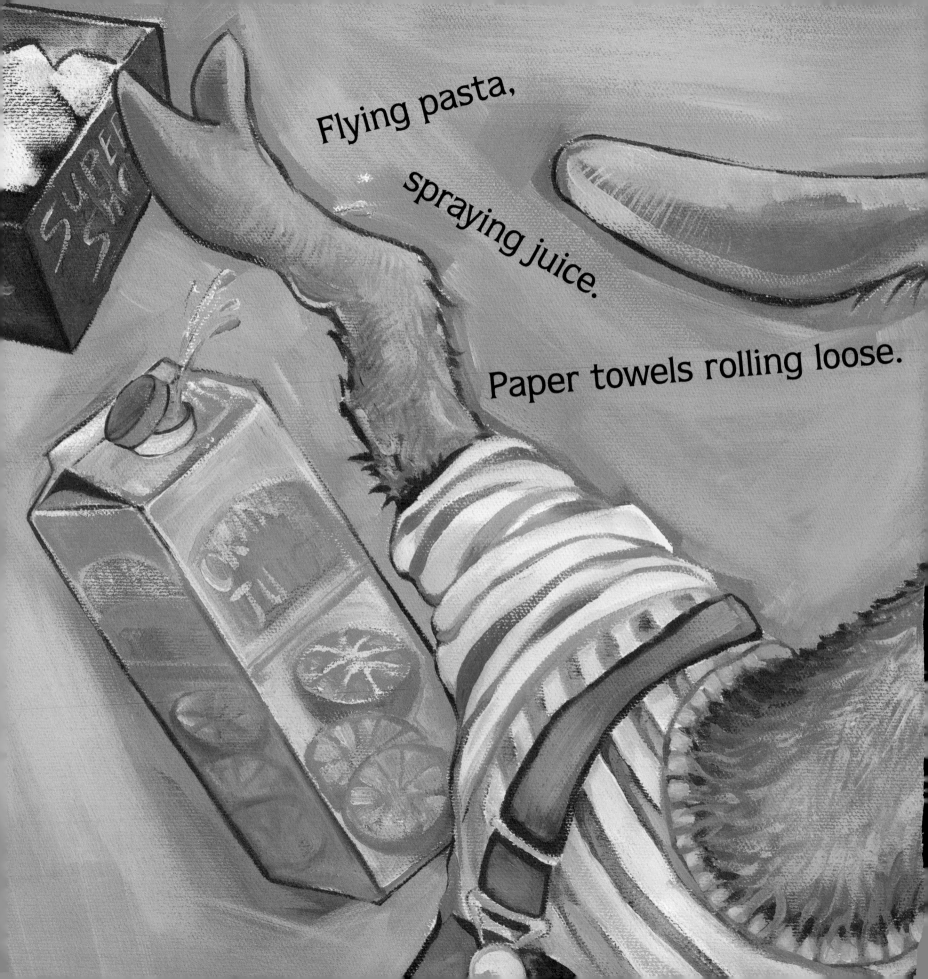

Coffee, bread, and chips galore. Shoes and sweaters hit the floor.

CRASH the cart and **SMASH** the signs.
No more waiting! **No** more lines!
Out go socks and Cheezee Puffs. . . .

Llama Llama,
that's enough!

Please stop fussing, little llama.
No more of this **llama drama.**
I think shopping's boring, too—
but at least I'm here with **you.**

Let's see if we can make this fun **and** get the llama shopping done.

Let's be a team at Shop-O-Rama—
Llama Llama shops **with** Mama!

Sweep up pasta,
mop up juice.
Wrap up towels rolling loose.

Pick up puffs and find the socks.
Put the shoes back in the box.

Push the cart with Mama Llama,
almost done at Shop-O-Rama.

Time to leave.
The shopping's done.
No more waiting.
Time for fun.

Out to parking, not too far.
Where did Mama leave the car?

Snap the buckle,
grab the box.
Put on brand-new
shoes and socks.

Say good-bye to Shop-O-Rama.

Llama Llama
loves his mama.

For Cordelia, my shopping buddy

ISBN-13: 978-0-545-15933-3
ISBN-10: 0-545-15933-4

12 11 10 9 8 7 6 5 4 3   9 10 11 12 13 14/0

Printed in the U.S.A.   08

This edition first printing, January 2009

Set in ITC Quorum

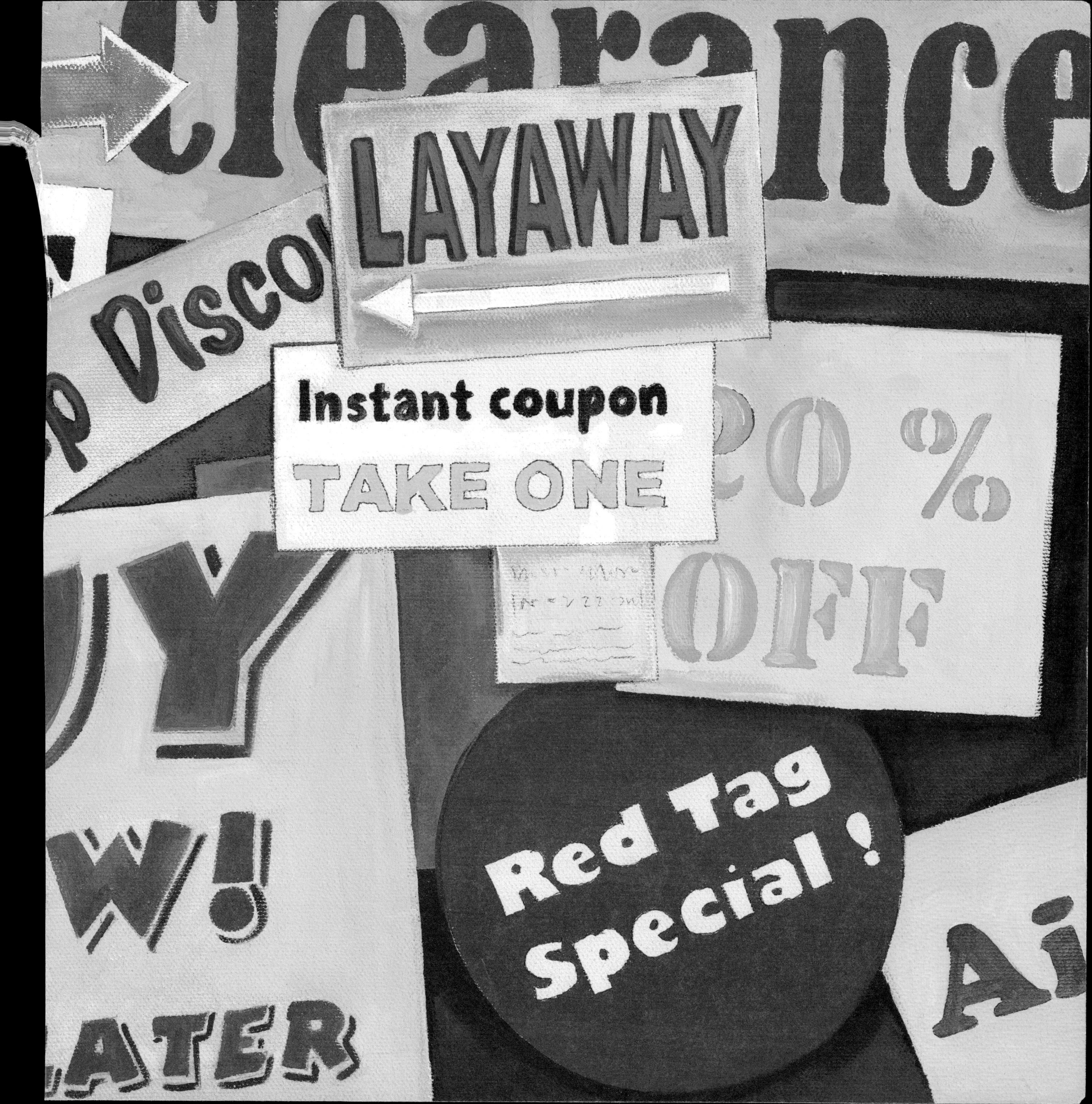
LAYAWAY
Instant coupon
TAKE ONE
OFF
Red Tag Special !